AVI is the honored author of 16 books for young people. He won the 1981 Christopher Award for *Encounter at Easton*. A librarian at Trenton State College, he often performs readings of his books in schools and libraries.

Avi is the father of two teen-age sons—both soccer players—and lives in Pennsylvania.

S.O.R. LOSERS

AVI

AN AVON CAMELOT BOOK

For Henry

AVON BOOKS
A division of
The Hearst Corporation
1790 Broadway
New York, New York 10019

The Bradbury Press edition contains the following Library of Congress
Cataloging in Publication Data:

Avi, 1937–
S.O.R. losers.
  Summary: Each member of the South Orange River seventh-grade
soccer team has qualities of excellence, but not on the soccer field.
    1. Children's stories, American. [1. Soccer—Fiction]
I. Title.
PZ7A.953Sab   1984   [Fic]   84-11022

First Camelot Printing: September 1986

Contents

How I Made the Team

"Where's Kelly?" Mr. Lester's face was very pale. "How can we practice without Kelly? Doesn't anyone know where he is? It's two-thirty."

Mr. Lester, our history teacher. I thought he might cry. For myself, I felt like laughing, laughing hysterically.

We were standing back of our school near the playing area, eleven of us, feeling very silly in brand-new red shorts and yellow T-shirts with "S.O.R." on our backs. If any dog catchers had come around they would have swooped us up for a bunch of stray mutts. Everywhere else on the field kids were running, tossing, kicking, all that stuff.

So far during two practices we had done two things. Since none of us knew the rules, Mr. Lester read them to us. Then we ran around in circles while he read the rules again, to himself. He didn't know them either. Second practice? We just tried kicking the ball. Wasn't easy.

"Gentlemen," pleaded Mr. Lester. "We have our first game tomorrow. Doesn't anyone know *something* about Kelly?"

No one said a word. The truth was going to hurt and no one wanted to hurt Mr. Lester. He was a nice guy.

"We have to play tomorrow," he said, as if we didn't know. We knew it too well.

It was my special buddy, Saltz, who let it out. "He no longer goes to our school. His father's job was transferred somewhere. Kelly kind of tagged along." I don't think we had our new uniforms on for more than thirty minutes, but Saltz, a natural slob, looked like he'd slept in his for twenty years. And he, like the rest of us, was only twelve.

"No longer in school?" said Mr. Lester, who had actually volunteered to be our coach. "But what about our game, our first game?"

"He wanted to be with his family," said someone. I think it was Eliscue.

The coach sighed. He was a history teacher, and we were not what they write history about. If South Orange River Middle School had a worse collection of athletes than the eleven of us, they were already on display in the museum mummy section. But there we

2

were, Hays, Porter, Dorman, Lifsom, Saltz, Radosh, Root, Barish, Eliscue, Macht and me, Sitrow. In a school that was famous, positively famous, for its teams and all-stars, we were not considered typical.

"Who did he think was going to be goaltender?" asked Mr. Lester. "Doesn't he understand, you can't play soccer without a goaltender. He should have told me." He said that just the way he might explain the sinking of the Titanic.

"His father probably got the job because Kelly didn't want to play," said Dorman.

When Mr. Lester got red in the face from frustration, he looked like an overripe tomato. His round face puffed and the few bits of topside hair were like old, dead leaves. It was clear he regretted being coach just as much as we regretted the thought of playing.

For example, me. I was so bad I was designated as the one sub. I didn't expect to play at all. But then, none of us expected to play. The thing was, our school had a requirement that you had to play at least one team sport each year you were there. We had slipped through the first year. None of us had played. None of us wanted to. But once they caught on, they made up a team for us, fast.

"Let's go back to the locker room," suggested Mr. Lester, who, I guess, needed to think things over.

Just as glad to skip practice, we followed him. Luckily, the locker room was empty. Everyone else was either playing or practicing.

I sat on a bench next to Saltz.

"Let's hear it for Kelly," he whispered.

"Maybe they'll call the whole thing off," I thought out loud.

He shrugged. Saltz and I had been pals since kindergarten. So I knew what he'd rather be doing: writing some of that poetry he likes.

"How many do we have here?" asked Mr. Lester.

"Two," said Root. He was our math genius.

"Gentlemen," said Mr. Lester, "this is not a joke. Please line up."

Our cleats clicking like bad pennies on the cement floor, we went up against the wall, all eleven of us. Porter was on one side of me, Saltz on the other.

"Maybe we'll get shot," said Porter.

"Only if we're lucky," said Saltz.

"Please, gentlemen, quiet," said Mr. Lester. He stood there looking miserable. You could tell he didn't like what he saw. But then, considering what we saw in the future, starting the next day, we didn't like it either.

"Gentlemen," he said softly. When Mr. Lester shouted, his voice got softer. "Gentlemen, you know why you're here."

No one said a word. Seventh-grade boys don't make good farewell speeches, not in front of execution squads.

"Do you?" he asked. My guess is that he was wondering himself.

"It's good for us," Lifsom said, as if describing someone's need for a head transplant.

"South Orange River Middle School has a fine sports tradition," continued Mr. Lester. "'Everybody plays, everybody wins.'" That's the motto of our program. And you, gentlemen, have been here a full year without being on any team."

"That's because we've got better things to do," said Barish.

Mr. Lester's face got positively purple. But he went on, believe me, softer. You had to strain to hear. "That's exactly the point. You are all—each one—nice, smart boys. You have, however, avoided sports. Too much desk work."

"Computers," slipped in Root. "The future."

Mr. Lester's face made the ultimate transformation. He turned deathly white, and spoke as though from the grave. "S.O.R. believes in the whole person. We've created this team for your good. From now on you're going to play. Sports is a major part of American life. Starting tomorrow we've got a season to play. Six games. Let's do it with honor."

"What about ability?" asked Dorman.

Mr. Lester passed over that point with a sigh. "We need a goaltender." I could see his eyes travel up and down the line. To my horror, they landed on me.

"Ed," he said to me, the way a kindly pirate might ask the next victim to walk the plank, "you're tallest. You'll be goaltender."

"Me?" I said, pointing to my narrow, weak and un-formed chest. I couldn't believe it.

"Yes, you."

"Sir," I said in a panic. "I never played goalie before. I never played soccer before. I never played *anything* before."

"Neither have your teammates. But we are going to give it our best, aren't we? We'll gain pride by trying. Now, gentlemen, you all have permission to be out of your classes in the afternoon. Be ready, here, tomorrow at one-thirty for the bus. In uniform. We don't want to be late. It makes for a poor start."

And that's how I became goalie for the South Orange River Middle School Special Seventh-Grade Soccer Team. I happened to be tallest.

Talk about talent.

On second thought, I'd better not. Not when you see what happened.

The Worst Team Meets the First Game

The ride to Buckingham Junior High's soccer field the next day was strange. We were not the only team going. Two other teams, our regular eighth-grade team as well as the sixth-grade soccer team, were on the bus. Everyone sat with his own group. They were all moody, worried, like they were playing the game in their heads. As for us, we were relaxed, looking out windows, passing jokes, talking about this and that. I mean *nobody* wanted to even think about what was going to happen.

Then, when we arrived, the other kids jumped to their feet all excited with much laughing, shouting, pounding each other on backs, like they wanted to get out. Now it was our turn to sit moody and glum.

The bus driver turned around and looked at us.

We were the only ones left. "Hey guys, this is it."

"Can't we go to the next stop?" asked Porter.

The bus driver thought the remark was a joke. We didn't.

So it was that on a chilly and gray September afternoon we stepped from the bus and slouched toward the Buckingham field. The leaves were just beginning to turn. Our stomachs already had. Right then and there I became opposed to capital punishment. I not only wanted to live, I firmly believed I was innocent.

We all were. Our only crime was that we didn't like sports much. Worse, we actually preferred other things. Not everything. Some things. For example, Saltz was keen on his writing, and only okay in biology. Lifsom was gung-ho about art, but his grades were generally just so-so.

So it went. Fairly normal. Or so we thought. Watching football games, rooting for teams, stuff like that, just wasn't important to us. True, Macht was a whiz at poker, and claimed that was a sport, but he didn't get much support. You'd think not being into sports was antihuman, or worse, un-American. Well, the world was about to get revenge.

And how? By the general notion that we were going to have *fun*.

Fun. It reminded me of a class trip to the A.S.P.C.A. Someone asked a woman there if they ever had to kill an animal. "Oh, no," she said with this ripe smile, "we just put them into a long, long sleep."

After two practices we could tell that we were heading into a long, long sleep.

When we got to the field, the Buckingham team was already lying in wait.

Mr. Lester went to speak to the other coach. Maybe to warn him. As he left, he said, "Get yourselves ready."

Get ready? Get lost is what we wanted to do.

Out in the middle of the field the referee was showing off, kicking the soccer ball up in the air with alternate feet, never once letting it touch the ground.

We watched.

"Think he's open to a bribe?" wondered Macht.

"Why not just get him for our team," Saltz said.

"Do an exchange," offered Radosh. "We'll ref. He'll play."

"Sure," said Porter, "but then we'd have to know the rules."

Porter had a point.

Then we watched the Buckingham team. They were kicking the ball about to each other as if it were on a guide wire.

"I think they know how to play," said Root, clearly upset by the possibility.

"Maybe we should ask for lessons, instead of a game," put in Dorman.

With that we all started to laugh. And couldn't stop.

Mr. Lester hurried back. When he saw us in the

midst of our fit, he got worried. "Is something the matter?" he asked.

"Root here," said Hays, "had this idea that we were going to play those guys. It broke us up."

"Why, yes," said Mr. Lester, perfectly serious. "They are the opposing team."

"What are they, all-stars?" asked Eliscue.

"Oh, no," said Mr. Lester, alarmed. "It's their third-string seventh-grade team. Perhaps, gentlemen, you should warm up."

"When you're cold, you're cold," said Root. It was such a bad joke we stopped laughing.

"Does everybody know what position he is playing?" asked Mr. Lester.

We did, sort of. During the second practice, book in hand, he had placed us around, but I wasn't sure of the position names, except goaltender.

"Now," said Mr. Lester, "remember the important thing is to . . ." Then, so help me, he forgot what he was going to say. But Mr. Lester was, if nothing else, prepared. Right off, he went to his pocket and pulled out some papers. Notes. "Ah, yes," he said, and began to read. "It's important to concentrate. Learn to meet the ball. And, gentlemen, the most important thing of all is . . ."

We never did learn the most important thing of all. The referee blew his whistle.

The Buckingham team gathered, their blue jerseys merging into a storm cloud. Out came a thunderous cheer.

If that cheer was meant to show us that, although a third-string team, they were real and strong and feeling victorious, that we had every reason to expect defeat, it worked.

"How about us doing a cheer?" suggested Mr. Lester.

"Shazam," said Lifsom. Not only was he the only one who said anything, it didn't work. We were still us.

3

●

First Blood (and Gore)

We sort of backed onto the field. Lifsom, who was playing up front in the middle, shook hands with the opposite Buckingham players. Maybe they decided to be nice to us. Anyway, it was our ball for starters.

As for myself, I was strolling around in the goal area trying to remember anything, which wasn't much, about the rules. How far could I go? I felt certain I could kick the ball, but on second thought, as well as third on to the seventh, I wasn't sure. Was I allowed to touch the ball with my hands, or just my elbows? Did knees count? Things like that.

In fact, I was pacing along the newly chalked goal lines, back to the field, when the whistle blew. I looked up, wondering what had gone wrong. What had gone wrong was, the game had begun.

Now the way it works, I think, or is supposed to work, is that Lifsom, being up front and middle, sort of kicks the ball back toward our side—at the moment it was Barish who was behind him—and away we would go.

But to give you a full sense of how the game went, all I can say is that somewhere, somehow, between the time the ball touched Lifsom's foot—I think it was his foot, because, as I said, I hadn't been watching—and the time it was supposed to reach Barish, Buckingham had already stolen the ball.

They didn't just steal it. They kept it. Forever. When I looked up, I saw this wall of storm-blue shirts rolling down the field, *in my direction*!

As for our guys, the ones in the red and yellow, they were doing one of four things:

Standing around.

Running the wrong way.

Backing up, furiously.

Falling down.

Or, actually, five things, because some people did a combination of two of the above, like Macht, who backed up, *and* fell down.

Anyway, you know how it is in history—battles and things—wars can truly be lost at the first shot. I understand that personally. I was at one.

Playing in front of me was Saltz, my special buddy. We not only grew up together, we lived near each other. Defended each other. Loved each other. So when he saw that advancing line of Buckingham blue attacking, attacking me, he actually did something.

First, he turned red in the face. A great red blotch. Then he started to charge at that blue line. Now, unlike me, Saltz is a big guy. With his T-shirt flapping all over the place, his arms flapping other places, his longish hair flapping in the remaining places, he *charged*.

What a sight!

For just a moment the blue line hesitated. I mean Saltz is a big guy. And the red face, the flapping, and so on . . .

The ball was squirting forward.

Saltz, I saw, was aiming right for it. My stomach, which had been traveling somewhere in the region of my throat, began to go right. I could see that Saltz was about to send that ball a billion miles in the other direction.

Except . . . he missed.

Honest, he did. He charged like a mad bull, cocked his leg, or whatever you do with your leg, kicked out, missed and kept right on going. He went, in fact, past all the Buckingham players before he realized what had happened.

And what had happened was that there was nothing between me, that ball and Buckinghams. The ball was coming right at me. I should know—I saw it trickle past me into the net.

It was only fifteen seconds into the game. But, to

tell the truth, that first few seconds was typical.
Final score:

BUCKINGHAM: 32
SOUTH ORANGE RIVER: 0

Or, in case you hadn't noticed, we lost our first game, badly.
We were on our way.
Down.

4

Heading Home

We got back on the bus feeling stupid. It wasn't just that we lost, but we lost by being so amazingly bad. Beyond belief. It had stopped being fun about two seconds into the game. It wasn't even a question of how good they were. We stank.

We were the first team to get back to the bus.

"Well," said the bus driver with lots of good cheer, "how'd you guys make out?"

"Lost," said someone.

"But close, I bet," said the driver.

"Distant," came the reply.

"Well, next time," was the driver's hope.

Then it was Mr. Lester's turn. "Gentlemen," he said, taking a quick look over his shoulder to make sure we were still alone, "I want to tell you how proud I am of you. You didn't give in."

"I bet he admired World War Two kamakaze flyers too," whispered Saltz into my ear. "The suicide guys."

"You kept up your spirits," continued Mr. Lester.

"Nothing else to keep up," said Radosh.

"You showed courage and character."

"What about talent?" called out Porter.

"Or skill?" Dorman offered.

Mr. Lester pressed on. "Each week, from experience and practice, you'll get better. I know you will. You have nothing to be ashamed about. Their coach told me he was impressed."

"With what?" asked Macht.

Mr. Lester said nothing.

"Mr. Lester," Hays called out. "How come, by the end of the game, they only had four men on the field? Is that legal?"

Mr. Lester blushed. "They were being sporting," he murmured and quickly sat down.

"Sporting?" said Saltz to me. "If they really wanted to give us a chance, they should have *all* gotten off the field. Those four guys scored five goals."

"What makes you think, if they had none, we would have scored *any*?" asked Radosh.

No one answered.

Then our other teams came on. One team had won. They were crazy happy. The other team tied. They were just dumb happy. Naturally, they wanted to know what happened to us. It was Hays who told them.

At first they didn't believe it. "No, really? What

17

was the score? Tell it straight." Things like that. After a while they had to believe. And they were amazed. Stunned. In awe. For a bit, anyway.

Then quickly it became joke time. Like, "Maybe if you hadn't shown up they would have scored less." There was some logic to that.

But it got so bad the coaches made them shut up and our team kept its distance. Untouchables.

By the time we got back to school we, at least, were into our usual kind of stuff: school gossip, homework, a special trip that was being planned. And the big thing—that we were going to work with partners for our history projects. We kept talking about who we wanted to work with, whom we didn't. The deal was, we were going to draw names out of a hat.

I mean, we had lost. Who cared? There were better things to think of.

Fortunately, when we got back to school we had to rush for our buses, so there wasn't much teasing.

That night, at dinner, my ma asked, as she usually did, how my day was.

"Fine," I said.

"Anything interesting?" Dad wanted to know.

"In history," I said, "we're starting on Indians. We're going to do projects and we get to work with someone."

"Who are you with?"

"Don't know yet," I said, but to be honest, I couldn't wait to get to school the next day to find out.

18

My Skills Are Rewarded

Next morning, though, when I walked into my classroom, there, on the board, in huge numerals it read:

32 – 0!

"Who wrote that?" I wanted to know.

"What?" asked Ms. Appleton who was my home room teacher.

"*That!*"

She looked at the numbers as if she hadn't noticed them before. "I have no idea. Does it mean something?"

"Sort of," I admitted, going right to my desk and dumping my books.

"Aren't you going to tell me?"

"I'd rather not."

In bits and pieces the rest of the class came in. Every time one of my teammates showed up—there were four in my room, Saltz, Porter, Lifsom and Hays—they looked at what was on the board. I could see them shrug and lower their shoulders a little.

Class came to order.

"Ms. Appleton, what's that mean?" asked one of the girls, the gifted, talented and excessively beautiful Lucy Neblet.

"I have no idea. Edward (she meant me) seems to know, but he's not telling. Or will you?"

I hadn't exactly enjoyed losing the day before. But, except for learning what I'd known already, that sports was not my thing, I hadn't spent a lot of grief on it. Yet when Lucy Neblet asked her question, all of a sudden, I felt *bad*. Like I had done something wrong, or dirty.

I looked around at Saltz, who sat next to me. He was looking down.

"Edward?" persisted Ms. Appleton.

"Our special soccer team—first game—we lost by that score," I managed to get out.

There was a moment of real shocked silence.

"Thirty-two to nothing!" hooted Hamilton, who was all-universe at *everything*.

From somewhere in the back of the room came a giggle. It caught on. Laughs. Big yuks. A grand old time. Except for the five of us who were on the team. I felt lower than a mole hole.

"I'm sure you'll do better next time," said kindly Ms. Appleton.

"They couldn't do worse!" bellowed Hamilton.

I felt like belting him in the mouth.

But the bell clanged and we started history, my favorite subject. It was then that we got to pick our project partner's name out of a hat. Who should I get but Lucy Neblet. Rather she got me, because she pulled out my name. Naturally, I didn't want to show that it was amazingly fantastic with me, but I was sky high. I couldn't have cared less about soccer.

Then, in the lunchroom, a couple of people came up to me—Saltz and I were talking about Lucy—and these guys asked me if it were true, about the game, that is.

"Yeah, sure," I said, like, "Don't bother me." But it did mean that word was getting around. Sure enough, from then on, all during lunch, I had this feeling that people were looking over at me, and giggling. More than once I'm sure I heard, "Thirty-two to zip."

I tried to be cool by just ignoring it all. If I thought about it, it would have interfered with the enjoyment of my tuna fish, banana and peanut butter sandwich, a real work of art which I make for myself each morning.

Then this big eighth-grader came up to me. "Hey, super-star, this is for you." He handed me a note. I gave him a dirty look and expected the worst until

I saw it was a message that I was to see Mr. Lester.

Mr. Lester was working in his classroom, alone.

"Ah, Ed," he said. "Please, sit down."

I glanced at his desk. Usually, it was loaded with history books. The American Civil War was his thing. It was neat to hear him talk about it.

But this time all I saw were books about soccer. That upset me. He was taking things seriously. Sure enough, he smiled. "I hope you weren't too troubled about yesterday," he said.

"No way," I said. "Why should I be?" but I sensed that I was being pushed that way.

"We took quite a licking."

"Somebody has to lose," I said. "The South lost."

"Listen, Ed," he said, waving his hands over his books. "I've been studying. We can make some adjustments. But that's not what I wanted to see you about. It's recommended here—now, where was it . . ." He began to leaf through one of the books. "Oh, it doesn't matter. What we need—it says—we should have a captain. You would make an admirable one." He held out his hand to congratulate me. "You are our captain."

"Me?"

"You're our best player. You can set an example.'

"Me. The best?"

"I saw you block a shot."

I felt like saying that, one: it had been an accident, and two: I didn't even remember doing it. Instead, I went out of the room feeling positively sick.

22

Me. Best player. Captain . . . Good grief. The thought of a slow jog through Death Valley at high noon was much more appealing.

That night, to set my mind straight, I called Lucy. We had a long talk about our project. Well, rock bands, mostly, but we began about the project.

Then I called Saltz and had a long conversation about my long conversation with Lucy.

There were still some nice places in my life.

How We Practiced

The word must have come down from somewhere,
for Mr. Lester called an extra practice. No one
wanted to go. It meant giving up our one free period.
Still, we had no choice.

As it turned out it was really a nice day, sort of
golden warm, so it wasn't bad to be out. Mr. Lester
led us to a place where, I think, no one could watch
us.

First he asked us to sit down.

"Now, gentlemen," he said, "we have to think
about this game more seriously."

Saltz shot up his hand.

"Yes, Saltz?"

"Why do we have to take it seriously?"

Mr. Lester blinked. "Because . . . we do. There's

nothing wrong about losing. It's just that we shouldn't lose by so much."

"What's the difference?" asked Hays. "Isn't a mile as good as a miss?"

Mr. Lester grew thoughtfully quiet. We waited for an answer. "It's a question of attitude," he began. "During the American revolutionary war, Americans lost lots of battles, but they didn't give up."

"Could you give us an example," I asked, taking my job as team captain to heart for the first time.

Mr. Lester perked up. "Well, yes, many of them. Consider the Battle of Bunker Hill . . ." And on he went, about how the Americans got their fort set up at night. How the British came by boat. How they stormed up the hill and what our side did. "Don't shoot till you see the whites of their eyes," and all that. It was really nifty the way he told it. And when he was done, he said, "So you see, even though the Americans retreated, it was, in a way, a great victory."

"Anything like that happen during the Civil War?" I wanted to know.

Again he wasted good time by thinking. "Actually, the Battle of Gettysburg was one in which no one truly won either, but because of that . . ." And he was off again, maybe even better than the first time around.

We just stayed put, happy to let him talk while the sun came on warm. By the time General Lee retreated the hour was almost gone.

He suddenly looked at his watch. "My goodness," he said. "We've used up most of our time."

"What about the Spanish-American War?" asked Radosh quickly.

Mr. Lester blinked. I felt for him. I could see he really wanted to tell us. Instead, with a sigh, he said, "Why don't you run around the field a couple of times."

That was okay. We pulled ourselves up and began to trot around at an easy, lazy pace. We did it twice and then came back to where Mr. Lester was waiting for us.

"Now what?" asked Barish.

"World War Two," offered Lifsom.

Mr. Lester, however, checked his watch. Even as he did we could hear the bell for class.

We didn't even wait. We sprang up and ran back to school. It was shop time and no one wanted to miss that.

As we went, I looked back over my shoulder. There was Mr. Lester standing under the tree, a bag of soccer balls on the ground. I almost felt sorry for him.

I'll say one thing though: it was the most interesting practice we had all season.

7 •

Second Game, First Goal

Our second game was at Shoreham. If South Orange River had a reputation for being great in sports, so did Shoreham. In fact, the schools were rivals. Not that I cared. I always did wonder who made up rivalries. The principals probably cooked them up.

We did get in another practice after the practice when we didn't practice. Wasn't bad. That is, I think we kicked the ball around a bit. I didn't think much about soccer because the next day we went to a big museum and saw a film—a really neat day.

In fact, on the bus to Shoreham, Saltz, Radosh and I got into this long discussion about some of the dinosaurs we saw in the museum. A guide told us no one knows exactly why they died off. We were trying to figure out why. Saltz had the best idea. "Probably got into sports," he suggested.

"Right," I said, "The Triceratops Toppers versus the Tyrannosaurus Tykes."

So by the time we got out of the bus at Shoreham, we were in a fairly good mood. Being in the bus alone helped. That happened because after the first game they gave us—and us alone—a small bus to use when we needed one. For the whole season. It was as if what we were doing might be catching.

As for my being captain, that hadn't amounted to much, except a little kidding. But, as we got near the field, Saltz slipped up to me and said, "Remember, the captain always goes down with his ship."

Actually, it was another beautiful day, one of those early fall days that makes you remember summer and wish it were back. Mr. Lester was all smiles. The team was loose. Positively jangling. As we closed in on the field, we could see the Shoreham players working out.

We got ourselves ready. Mr. Lester beckoned me over. "When the referee calls, you're supposed to go out and meet the opposing captain."

"What for?"

He looked blankly at me, blushing slightly. "I can't say I read that," he admitted.

After a bit, the referee did call. I went out to the middle. The Shoreham captain was a pretty big guy for a seventh grader, at least twice as wide as me. He held out his hand and we shook. He nearly busted my fingers.

"How's it going?" he said, dancing up and down with nervous energy like something was itchy in his shorts.

"Okay," I said, my fingers under my armpit to get some warmth back. "You got a nice field."

"Little chewed up from our last game."

"Oh? Who with?"

"Buckingham."

"Really," I said, pretending that was the least interesting thing in the world. "How'd you guys do?"

"We beat them, six zip."

"No kidding," I said, sorry I asked. In fact I decided that my first official duty as team captain was not to tell my teammates the truth.

Meanwhile, the ref was telling us he wanted a good, hard game, but no rough stuff. I felt like saying, "Don't worry, we do best at bad, soft and easy." But I didn't.

"Good luck," the Shoreham captain said to me.

"Thanks," I replied, "we'll need it."

He looked at me a little funny. Probably thought I was kidding. Ha-ha.

I can't tell you about the whole game. Just the highlights. Or rather, the lowlights. It wasn't all that different from the Buckingham game.

I do remember being impressed because they didn't score right away. Not in the first ten seconds, anyway. In fact, I think we had the ball on their side of the field briefly. But what is worth telling about is our first goal.

29

It came about this way.

They were on the attack. They were always on the attack. But in this case they had brought the ball nicely down the left line, passed it to the middle guys, pretty much in front of me—that is, in front of the goal.

Meanwhile, my trusty buddy Saltz, as well as Root and Hays, were right in there, flailing away, hacking with their feet, rear ends, heads, whatever they found useful and close to the ball. But the ball kept getting closer.

I crouched, ready to miss.

The ball squirted loose. Hays was right there and gave it a kick with the swift instinct of a true player. Right into *our* goal.

Point for them.

The best part was when the ball went in and the Shoreham team all lifted their arms. That's a soccer tradition, airing your armpits after all that footwork. Anyway, I saw Hays lift his arms too, with this great idiot's grin of success on his face.

Radosh tipped him off, delicately. "Wrong side, bozo," he said.

Hays' grin dropped like lead weights. He stood there, truly shaken.

Oh, well.

At another furious part of the game, I remember looking across the field and noticing that their goal-tender was lying flat on his back, hands beneath his head, taking a sun bath. That really made me mad. I was still glaring at him as their twenty-second goal went whizzing past my eyes.

Final score: 40 – 0.

Guess who won?

I wondered, did that make them better than Buckingham, or us worse?

"Well," said Dorman, as we dragged into our bus for the ride home, "they said we couldn't get worse, but we showed them. Lot of points."

"Yeah, but I scored one of them," Hays reminded us.

We applauded with slow, regular beats. "Yeh! Hurray!"

Mr. Lester, sitting up front with the driver, was doing his best to pretend he didn't know us by reading one of his books, *How to Be a Successful, Winning Coach*.

He never did tell me what a captain was supposed to do.

8

A Word from Our Sponsor

I knew we were heading into big trouble when every team member got a message—a *personal* message—from the principal, Mr. Sullivan. He wanted to see us during our lunch hour.

"What do you think he wants?" Dorman asked me. Since I had become captain, they asked me the cosmic questions.

"I think we're only going to be allowed to play third-grade teams," suggested Root, looking up from an electronic diagram that reminded me of robot guts.

"No such luck," I predicted.

Mr. Sullivan, the principal, didn't strike me as a sports guy. He was small, thin, pinched-up and tense. But his office seemed to be the storage room for all the trophies, ribbons, flags and whatnots that the school had ever won. I mean, you walked in there and you knew what was expected of you—to win.

"Well," Mr. Sullivan began with a smile. "So this is the special seventh-grade soccer team." It wasn't a sympathetic smile. More along the lines of an "I-don't-believe-it" smile.

"How's it going?" he asked.

"Could be worse," said Macht.

"Next game," agreed Barish.

"You're not going to give up, are you?" asked Mr. Sullivan. The way he said it you'd have to be a pervert to have answered "no."

"I suppose you think you're not very good," he said.

"Honesty is the best policy," said Eliscue.

"Well, you're new to the game," said Mr. Sullivan. "You have to have faith in yourselves. Not give up. I know you can do well. I just know it."

"How come you know," asked Saltz, "and we don't?"

Mr. Sullivan seemed taken aback. "I just do," he said.

"Any evidence?" asked Dorman.

The principal became very serious. "Boys," he said, "if you believe in yourselves, you can do *anything*." He gestured to the trophies, flags and ribbons. "Don't take a defeatest attitude. It will haunt you the rest of your lives. Do I look like an athlete?"

"No."

"Well, I run marathons, twenty-seven miles once a month. Now look at me."

We did. I didn't see any difference.

"How come you do it?" asked Porter.

"I like it."

"Well, we don't like this," Hays said.

"Besides, we stink," put in Radosh.

Mr. Sullivan shook his head. "As long as you want to believe that, you'll lose. What I'd like you to have is a brand-new attitude, the true South Orange River attitude: never accept defeat."

We hung our heads.

"Okay?" he said brightly. "Promise. Each of you, look me in the eye and promise."

I did, hard. And for the first time I noticed he was slightly cross-eyed. It took the edge off my promise.

He let us go then, telling us he'd come to one of our games to cheer us on.

Before splitting up we stood outside his office. "I'm beginning to think we might be an embarrassment to someone," said Saltz.

"Maybe he'll call the whole thing off."

We let that fond but empty hope cheer us.

"I think they want to teach us a lesson," I said.

"Which is?" asked Barish.

"I'm not sure I know yet," I admitted.

As we started to scatter I called after them, "Another game Friday. Sanger. Don't forget."

"I'm trying," shot back Dorman.

Saltz stayed by my side. "I made up a team poem," he said.

"You would."

"Want to hear it?"

"Do I have a choice?"

He pulled out his notebook and read:

> "*There once was a team from South Orange*
> >   *River,*
> *Who simply could never deliver.*
> *Given a way to choose,*
> *They always found new ways to lose,*
> *That marvelous, special, seventh-*
> >   *grade team from beautiful,*
> >   *successful, always winning*
> >   *and*
> >   *never losing,*
> >   *South Orange River.*"

"You and Shakespeare," I said.

"Think he was good in sports?" he asked.

"Sure, right field for the Bloomington Beer Nuts."

"They never do say, do they?"

The Third Game
and Other Disasters

Sanger took its turn. They came to our field. That meant we could have had a crowd of people watching. We did have a crowd, or rather a crowdette. A little girl came wandering by. She couldn't have known much of what was going on. To my eyes, she wasn't any older than five. And whatever she saw, she must not have liked. Either she was very smart or we were very obviously bad. Probably both. After ten minutes, she left. But by then we were losing by five goals.

Highlights of the game. Happily, I've managed to keep only one in mind.

In the second period, Macht took a nasty kick in the shins. Down he went, yelling, screaming, crying bloody murder. He was rolling on his back, holding on to his leg, trying to make sure it stayed there.

Now, as I've come to learn, what you're supposed to do is nothing. Ignore it. Play on. Hang tough. Be men.

Not us. I mean, the guy was our friend, even if he was great in math. Without even thinking about it, we all—and I mean all—rushed over and stood around trying to make him feel better.

The referee ran up to us, yelling that we were supposed to keep playing.

"He's hurt," I explained. Macht was, I admit, yelling softer by then.

"Ball's still in play!" cried the ref. "Ball's still in play!"

Sure enough, he knew something we didn't. They scored a goal. Walked it in. What did we care? It was only one of twenty-two.

Later, in the locker room, Mr. Lester called us to attention.

"Gentlemen," he said, "I think it's very kind of you to be concerned when a teammate gets hurt. But the game is such that you're not supposed to stop. Macht, you weren't hurt badly after all, were you?"

"No."

"He looked it," I said.

"Perhaps more startled than hurt," suggested Mr. Lester. "The thing is, they scored a goal."

"They scored lots of goals," Porter reminded him. "We've got only one Macht."

Mr. Lester sort of blushed, and sighed. "Tell me, gentlemen," he said, "are you getting any pleasure from this?"

There was a long, loud silence.

"*Any?*" he tried again.

"It's dumb," said Lifsom. "We stink. We really do. We're never going to win. Wouldn't it be better to just give up?"

Mr. Lester drew himself tall. He had a look I'd not seen before. I bet General Robert E. Lee had exactly that look when he sent his men on Pickett's charge up Cemetery Ridge at Gettysburg.

"Gentlemen," he said, "I want you to know, and I mean this sincerely, I believe in you. I do, truly." He actually made a fist. I never even knew Mr. Lester had one. "You can win!"

I had this uncomfortable feeling. "Why?" I wanted to know.

"Because you haven't given up."

"We'd like to," said Radosh.

"Gentlemen," cried Mr. Lester, "don't be losers. Be winners."

"I got an A-plus on my last math test," said Macht.

"Mr. Macht," said Mr. Lester, shouting in his smallest, lowest voice. "I'm talking about sports."

"Oh," said Macht.

"Three more games," said Mr. Lester. "Believe in yourselves."

In school the next day I was working on the history project with Lucy Neblet. We were hunched over this table, and having a good time. My notion of fun. Then out of nowhere, the school newspaper—which the kids make up—came fluttering down to cover our work.

"Hey!" I cried, looking up to see who did it. There was Cat-Face Charlie, a kid from class, who everyone knew had a crush on Lucy.

"What's the idea?" I said to him.

"Look!" he said, pointing at the newspaper and grinning.

I looked. On the front page, in headlines, it read:

NEW TEAM HAS WORST START IN SCHOOL HISTORY!

I turned. Lucy was looking at me sort of funny. All I could think was, "Three games to go."

The Facts of Life

If the story of what happened to us was in the movies, or on television, this is the point at which I think things are supposed to look up. You know, we would start to fight back. They wouldn't score all those points. Maybe one of us would drop dead from trying so hard that we'd vow to win, and would, crying for joy that the kid's death was worth what we'd win in the end: a plastic cup.

Well, this wasn't movies, television, or that series of romance books called "Lush Mush," which all the girls were reading. This was real.

For example . . .

Just a few days after the last game I was lying on my bed reading *The Light in the Forest*. I really liked it. Anyway, my father came into my room and sat on my desk chair. I could tell it was going to be a serious talk by the way he sat. When he wants to tell me I'm going to have to spend Saturday morning helping to clean house, he sits on the chair, regular. But when he straddles the chair, backwards, that means he's my pal and we're going to talk man-to-man.

He straddled my chair and looked around at all the slogans, pictures and bits and pieces I had picked up and stuck to the wall. I stayed where I had been, on my bed.

"How's it going?" he asked.

"Okay." My nose was still in the book.

"Got a minute?"

"Sure." I lowered the book, not knowing what was coming, except it was going to be heavy.

"How's school?"

"Fine."

"You really like it, don't you?"

"Most of it."

"When I went, I hated it."

"Sorry."

"Really hated it . . ."

"Well, I like it," I said. Then I suddenly had this wild notion that we were going to talk about *sex*! Trying not to show it, I got interested. I mean, we were due.

"Ed . . ." he said. "How's that soccer team you're on?"

"What?"

"The soccer team."

"Okay," I said, feeling shot down and wondering how he knew. I hadn't mentioned it.

"I didn't know you were on it, much less captain of the team. That's quite an honor. How come you never told us any of this?"

I shrugged. "It's no big deal. I have to play on a team. And Mr. Lester picked me for captain. Just the way he picked me to play goalie. I'm taller than the other guys."

"Better?"

"Taller. Saltz is better."

"Beefy."

"All muscle," I said loyally.

He looked at me, his eyes gone all shifty, so I knew some phoney questions were working their way up. Sure enough, he asked, "How's ah, the team, you know, coming along?"

"Fine," I said, picking up my book so he knew I had more important things to do.

"Yeah?"

I put the book down. "If you know the answers, how come you're asking?"

"You never told me one way or the other."

"Someone did."

"Well, that's . . . true." He was silent for a moment. "I . . . ah . . . gather you've not . . . won . . . anything."

"Nope."

"Close?"

"Light years."

"Ed . . ."

"Dad," I said, "you wouldn't be asking me this way if you didn't know the answers. What's on your mind? I have a lot of homework to do."

"I just thought . . . you know . . . I'm concerned about your team. Not just me, Ed. A bunch of bright guys like you. It's . . . your attitude," he blurted out. "You and the rest of the guys."

"How do you know?"

"I had a call from Mr. Tillman, the school counselor.

"You're kidding!"

"I did. And he's worried about you and the rest of the boys on the team."

"How come?"

"I just told you, your attitude."

"Because we get beaten?"

"Because you don't seem to care."

"What are we supposed to do? Cry? Sulk? Put our fists through lockers? Take dope? Go see Mr. Tillman and tell him we hate our fathers? Dad, we didn't want to be on a team. We *had* to be. We stink. So what?"

He shook his head. "That's being a quitter."

"How can you accuse me of quitting when I didn't want to join. If a guy breaks out of a torture chamber, is he a quitter? I mean, I do want to quit. We all do."

"Ed!"

"I don't want to talk about it."

After a few moments, he said, "A few of the dads were talking about this thing at the parents' meeting last night. We're going to hold some extra practices. Mr. Lester is all for it."

I threw my book down in disgust. "When?"

"Saturday mornings."

"No way."

"Yes."

"I'm supposed to go to the library with Lucy this Saturday to work on our project."

"Who's Lucy?"

"A friend!" I said fiercely.

He stood up. "Nine-thirty, fella. Havelock Field. You're team captain. You've got to set an example." He walked out of my room.

I called Saltz. "Guess what?" I said.

"Havelock Field. Nine-thirty. Saturday," he replied. "I'm strongest. I have to set an example."

"I don't believe it."

"For sure."

"What else did your folks say?"

"That we were a disgrace."

"Frig it . . ."

"You going?" he asked.

"Don't seem to have much choice."

"See ya," he said.

"Right," and I hung up the phone. I was beginning to feel like a cancer under attack. After a moment I called Lucy.

"Lucy? This is Ed. I can't work on our project Saturday morning."

"Why?"

"Soccer team. I've got to practice being a hero."

"I understand," she said, which made it worse. I was hoping she wouldn't.

World War I, Part II

I won't even describe that Saturday practice. All I'll say is that the fathers were serious. My idea of a good practice was that time when Mr. Lester told us about the Battle of Bunker Hill and the Battle of Gettysburg. Our fathers practiced us as if we were going into a battle of our own.

We hated it.

I don't even want to think about it.

Anyway, that week we were going to play Hopewell. When I woke up on the morning of the game it was raining like crazy. "Great," I thought. "They'll cancel."

At breakfast my mother said, "I thought I'd get out of work early and come watch you play."

"It's raining," I said.

"I won't melt."

"Don't you think they'll call off the game?"

"I certainly hope not," put in my father. "I'll come too. What's a little rain?"

"That's what they said when Noah began building the ark."

I would have gotten into more trouble if I said what else was on my mind. If I thought it might have kept me out of the game, I would have. More likely it would have only meant a grounding, and since the ground was already under water, I kept my mouth shut.

Worse, my father was right. They *didn't* call off the game. We got into uniforms and raincoats. What a combo. At the field it was cold, wet, muddy and very, very stupid.

Mr. Lester gave us one of his usual dynamic talks. "Gentlemen, this will be a true test of your characters. Conditions are terrible. It was either play or forfeit. We voted to play."

"We old enough to vote?" asked Saltz.

Mr. Lester, like all losing generals, ignored advice from his ground troops. Instead, he merely shifted his umbrella from one hand to the other. "Give it your best," he suggested, "your *true* best."

"We have," said Dorman. He sounded bitter.

"Make us proud," our noble coach urged.

"And *us* miserable," I thought.

"Remember," said Mr. Lester as we swam out to the field, "they have it as bad as you do."

47

Maybe. The difference was they knew how to play the game. Probably even wanted to. We didn't. Oh, we went out there. We tried to play. Honest. And with a bunch of dripping fathers and mothers on the soggy sidelines sort of cheering us on, we gave it a shot. The shot carried four inches.

I've read books, a couple, about World War I. Trench warfare. It was nothing compared to our game. The whole field was like a bottomless mud pit. When we *began*, the muck was over my shoes. From there on, it got worse.

For example, when the ball came down, instead of bounding, it would hit with a humungous "*SPLAT!*" showering mud everywhere, and sticking wherever it touched. It got so waterlogged it was like kicking a cannonball.

Some lowlights. We were losing, naturally, by about twenty-one to nothing. I was already a little shellshocked. I didn't mind the trench warfare so much. But it was like they were using me for target practice.

There I was, leaping this way and that, like a wet cow trying out for the lead role in a Spiderman movie. It got so bad that after a while, when I looked up, I noticed our team had retreated into a kind of wet, human-wall, semicircle around our goal. As walls went, it wasn't exactly the Great Wall of China. More like Jericho when it kept tumbling down. Shots kept coming in.

Once, I took this great leap. Somehow I ticked the ball with my frozen fingers when it went into the net (making it thirty-two to nothing). I did have the satisfaction of seeing that at least the ball went in crooked. But then, when *I* came down in the muck I lost my wind. And all desire to get up. I just lay there in the mud and rain, relaxed and feeling curiously happy.

Next thing I knew Mr. Lester as well as my mother and father were squatting down over me.

"Ed! Ed! You all right?" I heard my mother cry.

I opened my eyes. For reasons I don't understand, they were trying to keep the rain off me. Why then?

"Are you all right?" asked Mr. Lester in that super-quiet voice he reserves for true panic.

I remembered: I was his *best* player.

"Sure," I said, perfectly calm. "I love this."

My father didn't like that. "Get up, Ed," he urged.

"It's safer here," I said.

That was the big difference between World War I and our game. After being shellshocked those guys got to go to Paris for a weekend of fun. I was told to be a target again.

My favorite memory of that afternoon, however, came a little later. I saw the ball come to rest in a puddle—actually the whole field was a puddle—this one was just a fathom or so deeper than everywhere else. The resting ball, however, brought Eliscue and Macht at a gallop, each running at the ball full-tilt, neither seeing the other.

They met that ball with a huge "*BONG!*" It must have been at the exact same moment, for the ball went *up*, I mean straight up, somewhere into the rain clouds.

The two guys just stood there, bewildered, turning around, back to back, one against the other, trying to figure out where the ball had gone. Well, since it went straight up, it came straight down. It hit them both on their heads at the same moment. And it was a heavy, waterlogged ball. Well . . .

Down they went, knocked out. Both of them.

Once again Mr. Lester ran out onto the field, umbrella in hand. I think Macht's ma was there too. When they got those boys up, they wobbled.

Somewhere around that time everybody agreed that since the U.S. Constitution forbids cruel and unusual punishment, and since we had yet to score even one goal that season, and there was only a little likelihood of our scoring a catch-up forty-two goals in the last five minutes of play, they would call it all off.

That night both my parents came into my room. "Ed," said my father, lifting the hot water bottle from my face.

"What?" I didn't even want to talk sex.

"We liked what we saw."

"That was mud you saw."

"I could see some improvement," said my father, hurt by my attitude. After all, he'd helped set up the extra practice.

"I couldn't see anything," I said, snuggling down under five blankets as I tried to get warm.

"Just believe in yourself, love," my mother all but chanted at me. "Believe in yourself and you can do it."

I closed my eyes and let my mind drift. Two games left. Well, I told myself, it couldn't get worse.

Which only goes to show how even I had gotten suckered into what they called *believing*.

It did get worse.

Some Sympathy
from Mr. Tillman

"I'd like to see a few people," said Ms. Appleton when class started a couple of days later. And she called up the five team members.

When she did, Hamilton laughed, as if we were an automatic joke.

"They going to be traded to the elementary school?" he called out. "For a player to be named later?" That made the class laugh, even Lucy Neblet.

The five of us somehow managed to get to the front desk.

"I think it's wonderful how you won't give up," Ms. Appleton said to us. Since we did want to give up, we looked at her blankly.

"I knew you were bright and hard working, all of you," she said. "I didn't know you had so much courage."

We hadn't noticed that either.

"I mean it," she said. "I'd like to come to your next game and cheer you on. Would you mind?"

"It's ugly," warned Lifsom.

"Sick," agreed Hays.

"Don't worry. You'll win," she said brightly.

"Why does everyone keep saying that?" I asked her.

"Because you work so hard. And when you work hard like that, you win." She said it with such a nice smile, I wanted to believe that too.

"When's your next game?"

"Thursday. Pennington."

"Do you mind if I come?"

"I could think of better ways to kill an afternoon," said Saltz.

Ms. Appleton giggled. Then she said, "Mr. Tillman wants to see you all."

"Now?" asked Porter. "I have my special reading project to work on."

"That can wait."

"I don't want it to wait," cried Porter.

"He's expecting you all," said Ms. Appleton, and that was the end of that.

So the five of us, pretty promptly because we wanted out of there, went to Mr. Tillman's office. The rest of the team was already gathered.

Mr. Tillman's office was a fairly small place, meant for only one loser at a time, not a whole team of losers. Still, we managed to squeeze in.

The walls were covered with cute posters selling

joy and happiness. It was depressing, as if you weren't allowed to be anything but happy, no matter what. For instance, there was a picture of a kitten about to drop down into the Grand Canyon, with the slogan, "Keep Laughing, Baby." Cats don't laugh.

Another was a picture of a kid with a big smile. The message read, "It Takes Less Muscle to Smile than to Frown." I had an image of some mad surgeon figuring that out. Some fun.

And then, Mr. Tillman was not my favorite. A great big, huge guy. Someone once told me he played football and tried to make it with the pros. And also, he was always dressed the same; turtleneck sweater and beads around his neck. A sixties flower child gone to seed. As it is, I never trust anyone whose neck is wider than his brains. That's a motto I made up. But I don't think Mr. Tillman would have put that slogan up in his office.

Anyway, he got us all in, then had us sit down on the floor and be uncomfortable. Really happy-like, he said, "How you guys doing!" For a small room, he talked big.

"Okay," said Radosh.

Mr. Tillman leaned forward. "*Honest?*"

"If you want the truth, Mr. Tillman," I said, "we aren't feeling very good."

"Right on!" said Mr. Tillman, jangling his beads. "Now we're talking *truth*! And you feel bad about it. Think miserable. Have bad dreams. Sense of defeat. Disappointment. Any bed wetting? Kids tease you about the games? Probably some of your parents yell at you for being so rotten all the time. Any of you guys have girlfriends?"

Eliscue, who'd had girlfriends from nursery school on up, raised his hand.

"She poke fun at you, never want to be seen with you?"

For the first time I saw Eliscue ashamed that he even knew girls.

"I know," continued Mr. Tillman, "you guys are starting to *hate* yourselves!"

"Mr. Tillman," I said, "what can you expect? All we get from people is, 'Keep on trying. You can win.' I mean, we keep disappointing them. I am beginning to hate myself."

"I *love* you for saying that, Ed," cried Mr. Tillman. "The trick is, do you believe in yourselves?"

"No way," said Saltz.

"Why not? Someone want to share his feelings with me?"

"Because we stink," said Dorman. There was a general murmur and nodding of approval.

"Nope," said Mr. Tillman, "I won't buy that. I won't let you run yourselves down. *I* believe you can do it. Let me share something with you guys. The trick is, you *must* trust yourselves."

"Don't you have to be good too . . . a little?" asked Barish.

Mr. Tillman shook his massive head. "Heart!" he cried, thumping that mass of body where I suppose he keeps his heart. His beads bounced and rattled.

"Mr. Tillman?" asked Porter.

"Yes?"

"I have this reading project. It's really important to me. May I go work on it now?"

Mr. Tillman looked sad, as if he had been insulted, or his mother and father had, or his sister, or maybe his whole family. "Boys," he said, "the bottom line is this, 'Don't avoid your responsibilities.'"

That was a new one.

"Learn to *accept* your responsibilities!" he bellowed. We all jumped. "Learn that, and it will all be worthwhile!"

There was some more. Just as loud. But mostly it added up to the same thing: we owed *them*.

"Wish they'd just let us lose in peace," said Hays when we got out.

"Oh, good grief," I said.

They looked where I was pointing. A big piece of brown paper had been put on the wall. In crude letters was written:

Support a Team In Big Trouble!
Special Seventh-Grade Soccer Team!

S.O.R. vs. Pennington
1:30
If we care — so will they!

We all had the same reaction. A quick check to see

who might be looking, and rip, down it came. Plus the seven others we found around the school.

When we got back to class I had the nerve to ask Ms. Appleton about those posters.

"A class project," she said sweetly. "We're going all-out to support you."

"Why?" I said, feeling sick.

"S.O.R. has no losers," she said firmly.

"Yeah," I said, "well, I believed in Santa Claus too, once."

We Score! Sort Of

The game against Pennington was, well, interesting. Great weather. Crisp and bright. It almost made me want to be there. Sure enough, there were a bunch of people who came to watch. Ms. Appleton brought the whole rest of my class. Some parents too. Mr. Sullivan was there. So was Mr. Tillman. I think he had on new beads for the occasion.

Mr. Lester had us over by a corner where, after we pretended to get ready, he gave us his talk.

"Now, gentlemen, Pennington isn't such a great team. They've won a few and lost a few. More like you guys."

"We didn't win any," Porter reminded him.

Mr. Lester looked toward the sidelines. "Today you will," he said.

"How do you know?" asked Dorman.

"I feel it."

"Where?" Radosh wondered.

"And what about tomorrow?" Lifsom wanted to know.

"Gentlemen," said Mr. Lester, "we can really turn the season around if you want. Why not win for those nice people who have come to cheer?"

"Let them do it for themselves," whispered Saltz.

"Now," concluded Mr. Lester, "come out fighting and keep on fighting." He made that pathetic fist of his.

Right from the start, we tried. Honest. We got together in a circle, touched hands and started to roar, except just when we began, Eliscue sneezed. So instead of screaming, "Fight!" what came out was: "Fi . . ." *Sneeze*! "God bless you." "God bless you." "Thanks."

Not what I'd call a mean team.

As for the game. Well . . . there were one or two things. The big moment was when we scored a goal. Really. It was the only score (for our side) so far that season.

I'd like to tell you that Porter brought it smartly down the right line, snapped a crisp clothesline shot to Lifsom, who brilliantly headed it back to Hays, who smashed it by the helpless, prostrate goalie . . . except it didn't happen that way.

As much as I could see of it, the goal came about when Lifsom was trying to get the ball out of our territory. Well, that time he actually got his foot on it. The ball even started to go in the right direction. An improvement.

But then one of their guys intercepted, dropping the ball along his body. Then he began running it back. Our side moved into automatic full retreat.

But somehow, their guy tripped. The ball got away. Dorman saw the ball free and got it moving deep into their turf. I could see how excited he was by the notion that he was actually on the move with not much between him and their goal except their goalie because of what he did. What he did was stop and watch.

Macht came up and—not wanting to waste a shot—we didn't get too many—stole the ball from Dorman (who might have fallen asleep for all he moved) and gave a boot. Only Macht topped the ball. The ball just squirted forward. And Macht fell down.

What happened next? Their goalie cracked up, laughed so much that he let that little dribbler of a ball keep coming.

Meanwhile, Radosh came up from the left and gave the ball a thump, again, right at their goalkeeper.

Their goalie punched it right back. It hit Hays on the head and bounced into their goal.

Mind, I didn't say Hays headed the ball in, I said the ball hit him on the head and bounced in. In fact, Hays was so dizzy from the shot that he was actually walking around in circles for a few minutes.

It figured: we finally score a goal and the guy who scored it never did know what happened.

From the reaction of the people on the sidelines—

our people—you would have thought we had just won the World Series. They went wild.

Actually, I was much more interested in the way Hays was wobbling all over, like a wasted duck. *That* was interesting.

As for the other high point, it involved me. It wasn't so complicated, but since it was me, I had the best view, sort of.

It came about because during the third period my shoe became untied. Normally, I'd wait for a lull in the action to re-tie it. However, there were no lulls, and as time went on I was sure my shoe was going to fall off. I had to do something. Over I bent to tie it. Only then the shoelace broke. That meant more work. And concentration.

What happened next was this terrible thud against my backside. It sent me head first into the net one way, and the ball another way, also into the net.

Buddy Saltz helped me untangle myself from the net. "It's probably not a bad idea to face the field," he suggested.

"Do you want to play goal?" I snapped.

"Not tall enough," he reminded me.

Final score: 18 – 1.

In the locker room there were some guys from our other teams. Of course they had to know what happened to us. We told them.

At first there were the usual jokes, and then this

guy, Roberts, who was captain of the eighth-grade first-string team, stood on a bench and yelled for quiet.

We all listened.

"Look here," he said, looking right at us. As usual we were bunched together for self protection. "The joke's over," shouted Roberts. "When are you jerks going to get your act together? You're making *us* look stupid!"

Fortunately, Mr. Lester came in just then. There might have been a riot. Anyway, Mr. Lester shooed us all over into a corner to give us some kindly pointers. Not that anyone listened. It had all gotten too frustrating.

Then Mr. Tillman burst in. "Listen up, you guys," he said to us. We gave him our attention. He would have taken it anyway. There was an angry glint in his eyes that suggested trouble.

"I think I've learned my lesson," he said. "I admit it. I tried to sweet-talk you guys into feeling better about yourselves. That was wrong. What you need to be told is how rotten you looked out there today. I've never seen worse. Not around here. And you need to hear something else. I've checked. In the history of South Orange River Middle School sports, no team, I repeat, *no team*, has ever lost *all* its games.

"Do you guys want to go down in history as the worst team? Do you?"

There was absolute, stunned silence.

"Do you?" He insisted on an answer.

"Odds on that we can," said Macht.

Mr. Tillman turned savagely. "That's a defeatest attitude, Macht. Can it!" and he stalked out.

Mr. Lester looked embarrassed. "I know you try," he said softly. "I appreciate that. But I think it would be good to win one game. Next we play Parkville. Our last game. And I think I should tell you something. Parkville hasn't won a game all season either."

With those words of encouragement he left us.

"My gosh," said Barish, "another team as bad as us."

"Awesome," said Dorman.

"We'll be playing for 'Worst in the Universe,'" said Radosh.

There was almost—not quite—a thrill of excitement.

Lucy

I was sitting in class trying to follow the math teacher who was working out a problem on the board. Looking down I discovered a carefully folded piece of paper on my desk with my name on it. A passed note.

I looked at Saltz. He shrugged.

Propping up my math book to hide my hands, I carefully unfolded the note. It read:

> *Meet me after lunch by*
> *the downstairs dump bins.*
> *Lucy*

Astonished, I slammed my elbow into Saltz and palmed the note to him. He looked at it and *he* turned all red.

I tried to squirm around to look at Lucy but all I got was the math teacher saying, "Ed, keep your eyes up here, will you? You need to know this. It might even help your team score goals."

Big yuks.

Anyway, all during the first part of lunch hour Saltz and I had a serious discussion about Lucy Neblet. As we stuffed sandwiches and Twinkies in our mouths, as well as sucking up milk through straws, the talk went something like this:

Saltz began by asking, "What do you think?"

"I don't know. I am working on that history project with her."

"What's that supposed to mean?"

"Doesn't mean anything."

"What's the project about?"

"Mohawk Indians."

"Did you ever see her sister?"

"Whose sister?"

"Lucy's."

"Yeah."

"Well?"

"Well what?"

"Just, well."

"That's all you think about."

"I wasn't thinking about anything."

"Yes you were."

"How do you know?"

"I just do."

"I wasn't."

"Then how come you asked?"

"Just wanted to know."

"So nosey."

"You like her?"

"Who?"

"You know."

"No, I don't."

"Do too."

"What's it to you?"

"Curious."

"Why, do you?"

"Me, what?"

"I just said."

"No way."

"You used to."

"So what?"

"Then, who?"

"Me to know and you to find out."

"You're crazy."

"So you do like her."

"Maybe."

"Think she likes you?"

"Don't know."

"Someone once told me if she winks at you that means she does."

"Who told you?"

"What's the difference?"

"I'm going."

"Tell me what she said."

"She hasn't said anything yet."

"Watch her eyes."

"See ya."

"See ya."

I got out of the lunch room by telling the teacher on duty that I had to go to the boy's room. Instead I went downstairs, my heart beating, my head thinking, "This is it," except, I had no idea what "it" was.

At the back of the stairwell were these big garbage bins. The place stank. It was sort of dark and mysterious. But there was Lucy, perky and pretty.

"Hi," I said.

"Hi," she returned.

That was all until I said, "What's happening?"

"You're captain of the special soccer team, aren't you?" She was whispering, as if we were about to pass secrets to the Russians.

"Yeah," I said to her question. Don't ask me why, but I whispered too.

"Well," she continued, "I just thought I'd tell you . . ." She stopped.

"Tell me what?"

Her eyes were cast down. "I'm sorry you're losing."

"What?"

She looked up. No winking yet. "I'm just very sorry that you're losing." Then she blinked *both* eyes.

Something inside of me started to boil. "Why?" I said for the millionth time. "Why?"

"Why what?"

"Why are you sorry?"

"I just am," she said, startled by my reaction. "You must feel so badly."

"Well," I said, "I'm glad we're losing." By then I was almost shouting.

She looked at me as if I was crazy.

"Because if everyone else in this whole school wants to win," I kept on, "we're the eleven most unusual people in the whole building. And I like it that way!" Turning, I started for the steps, yelling, "Let's hear it for losers!"

For all I know she just stayed there by the garbage bins. It was the end of a beautiful romance.

15
•

The Tension Builds

I should have guessed what was going to happen next when this kid from the school newspaper interviewed me. It went this way.

NEWSPAPER: How does it feel to lose every game?
ME: I never played on a team that won, so I can't compare. But it's . . . interesting.
NEWSPAPER: How many teams have you been on?
ME: Just this one.
NEWSPAPER: Do you want to win?
ME: Wouldn't mind knowing what it feels like. For the novelty.
NEWSPAPER: Have you figured out why you lose all the time?
ME: They score more goals.

NEWSPAPER: Have you seen any improvement?

ME: I've been too busy.

NEWSPAPER: Busy with what?

ME: Trying to stop their goals. Ha-ha.

NEWSPAPER: From the scores, it doesn't seem like you've been too successful with that.

ME: You can imagine what the scores would have been if I wasn't there. Actually, I'm the tallest.

NEWSPAPER: What's that have to do with it?

ME: Ask Mr. Lester.

NEWSPAPER: No. S.O.R. team has ever lost all its games in one season. How do you feel about that record.

ME: I read somewhere that records are made to be broken.

NEWSPAPER: But how will you feel?

ME: Same as I do now.

NEWSPAPER: How's that?

ME: Fine.

NEWSPAPER: Give us a prediction. Will you win or lose your last game?

ME: As captain, I can promise only one thing.

NEWSPAPER: What's that?

ME: I don't want to be there to see what happens.

Naturally, they printed all that. Next thing I knew some kids decided to hold a pep rally.

"What for?" asked Radosh.

"To fill us full of pep, I suppose."

"What's pep?"

Hays looked it up. "Dash," he read.

Saltz shook his head.

"What's dash?" asked Porter.

"Sounds like a deodorant soap," said Eliscue.

And then Ms. Appleton called me aside. "Ed," she said, sort of whispering (I guess she was embarrassed to be seen talking to any of us), "people are asking, 'Do they *want* to lose?'"

"Who's asking?"

"It came up at the last teachers' meeting. Mr. Tillman thinks you might be encouraging a defeatest attitude in the school. And Mr. Lester . . ."

"What about him?"

"He doesn't know."

It figured. "Ms. Appleton," I said, "why do people care so much if we win or lose?"

"It's your . . . attitude," she said. "It's so unusual. We're not used to . . . well . . . not winning sometimes. Or . . . or not caring if you lose."

"Think there's something the matter with us?" I wanted to know.

"No," she said, but when you say "no" the way she did, slowly, there's lots of time to sneak in a good hint of "yes." "I don't think you *mean* to lose."

"That's not what I asked."

"It's important to win," she said.

"Why? We're good at other things. Why can't we stick with that?"

But all she said was, "Try harder."

I went back to my seat. "I'm getting nervous," I mumbled.

"About time," said Saltz.

"Maybe we should defect."

"Where to?"

"There must be some country that doesn't have sports."

Then, of course, when my family sat down for dinner that night it went on.

"In two days you'll have your last game, won't you," my ma said. It was false cheerful, as if I had a terminal illness and she wanted to pretend it was only a head cold.

"Yeah," I said.

"You're going to win," my father announced.

"How do you know?" I snapped.

"I sense it."

"Didn't know you could tell the future."

"Don't be so smart," he returned. "I'm trying to be supportive."

"I'm sick of support!" I yelled and left the room.

Twenty minutes later I got a call. Saltz.

"Guess what?" he said.

"I give up."

"Two things. My father offered me a bribe."

"To lose the game?"

"No, to win it. A new bike."

"Wow. What did you say?"

72

"I told him I was too honest to win a game."

"What was the second thing?"

"I found out that at lunch tomorrow they are doing that pep rally, and worse. They're going to call up the whole team."

I sighed. "Why are they doing all this?" I asked.

"Nobody loves a loser," said Saltz.

"Why?" I asked him, just as I had asked everybody else.

"Beats me. Like everybody else does." He hung up.

I went into my room and flung myself on my bed and stared up at the ceiling. A short time later my father came into the room. "Come on, kid," he said. "I was just trying to be a pal."

"Why can't people let us lose in peace?"

"People think you feel bad."

"We feel *fine*!"

"Come on. We won't talk about it any more. Eat your dinner."

I went.

16

●

Full of Pep

Next day, when I walked into the school eating area for lunch there was the usual madhouse. But there was also a big banner across the front part of the room:

**Make the Losers Winners
Keep Up the Good Name of
S.O.R.**

I wanted to start a food fight right then and there.
I'm not going through the whole bit. But halfway through the lunch period, the president of the School Council, of all people, went to a microphone and called for attention. Then she made a speech.
"We just want to say to the Special Seventh-Grade Soccer Team that we're all behind you."

"It's in front of us where we need people," whispered Saltz. "Blocking."

The president went on. "Would you come up and take a bow." One by one she called our names. Each time one of us went up, looking like cringing but grinning worms, there was some general craziness, hooting, foot stomping, and an occasional milk carton shooting through the air.

The president said: "I'd like the team captain, Ed Sitrow, to say a few words."

What could I do? Trapped, I cleared my throat. Four times. "Ah, well . . . we . . . ah . . . sure . . . hope to get there . . . and . . . you know . . . I suppose . . . play and . . . you know!"

The whole room stood up to cheer. They even began the school chant.

"Give me an S! Give me an O . . ."

After that we went back to our seats. I was madder than ever. And as I sat there, maybe two hundred and fifty kids filed by, thumping me hard on the back, shoulder, neck and head, yelling, "Good luck! Good luck!" They couldn't fool me. I knew what they were doing: beating me.

"Saltz," I said when they were gone and I was merely numb, "I'm calling an emergency meeting of the team."

17

•

Secret Meeting

Like thieves, we met behind the school, out of sight. I looked around. I could see everybody was feeling rotten.

"I'm sick and tired of people telling me we have to win," said Root.

"I think my folks are getting ready to disown me," said Hays. "My brother and sister too."

"Why can't they just let us lose?" asked Macht.

"Yeah," said Barish, "because we're not going to win."

"We might," Lifsom offered. "Parkville is supposed to be the pits too."

"Yeah," said Radosh, "but we're beneath the pits."

"Right," agreed Porter.

For a moment it looked like everyone was going to start to cry.

"I'd just like to do my math," said Macht. "I like that."

There it was. Something clicked. "Hays," I said, "you're good at music, right."

"Yeah, well, sure—rock 'n' roll."

"Okay. And Macht, what's the lowest score you've pulled in math so far?"

"A-plus."

"Last year?"

"Same."

"Lifsom," I went on, getting excited, "how's your painting coming?"

"I just finished something real neat and . . ."

"That's it," I cut in, because that kid can go on forever about his painting. "Every one of us is good at something. Right? Maybe more than one thing. The point is, *other* things."

"Sure," said Barish.

"Except," put in Saltz, "sports."

We were quiet for a moment. Then I saw what had been coming to me: "That's *their* problem. I mean, we are good, good at *lots* of things. Why can't we just plain stink in some places? That's got to be normal."

"Let's hear it for normal," chanted Dorman.

"Doesn't bother me to lose at sports," I said. "At least, it didn't bother me until I let other people make me bothered."

"What about the school record?" asked Porter. "You know, no team ever losing for a whole season. Want to be famous for that?"

"Listen," I said, "did we want to be on this team?"

"No!" they all shouted.

"I can see some of it," I said. "You know, doing something different. But I don't like sports. I'm not good at it. I don't enjoy it. So I say, so what? I mean if Saltz here writes a stinko poem—and he does all the time—do they yell at him? When was the last time Mr. Tillman came around and said, 'Saltz, I *believe* in your being a poet!'"

"Never," said Saltz.

"Yeah," said Radosh. "How come sports is so important?"

"You know," said Dorman, "maybe a loser makes people think of things *they* lost. Like Mr. Tillman not getting into pro football. Us losing makes him remember that."

"Us winning, he forgets," cut in Eliscue.

"Right," I agreed. "He needs us to win for *him*, not for us. Maybe it's the same for others."

"Yeah, but how are you going to convince them of that?" said Barish.

"By not caring if we lose," I said.

"Only one thing," put in Saltz. "They say this Parkville team is pretty bad too. What happens if we, you know, by mistake, win?"

That set us back for a moment.

"I think," suggested Hays after a moment, "that if we just go on out there, relax, and do our best, and not worry so much, we'll lose."

There was general agreement on that point.

"Do you know what I heard?" said Eliscue.

"What?"

"I didn't want to say it before, but since the game's a home game, they're talking about letting the whole school out to cheer us on to a win."

"You're kidding."

He shook his head.

There was a long, deep silence.

"Probably think," said Saltz, "that we'd be ashamed to lose in front of everybody."

I took a quick count. "You afraid to lose?" I asked Saltz.

"No way."

"Hays?"

"No."

"Porter?"

"Nope."

And so on. I felt encouraged. It was a complete vote of no confidence.

"Well," I said, "they just might see us lose again. With Parkville so bad I'm not saying it's automatic. But I'm not going to care if we do."

"Right," said Radosh. "It's not like we're committing treason or something. People have a right to be losers."

We considered that for a moment. It was then I had my most brilliant idea. "Who has money?"

"What for?"

"I'm your tall captain, right? Trust me. And bring your soccer T-shirts to me in the morning, early."

I collected about four bucks and we split up. I held Saltz back.

"What's the money all about?" he wanted to know. "And the T-shirts."

"Come on," I told him. "Maybe we can show them we really mean it."

Back Words

When I woke the next morning, I have to admit, I was excited. It wasn't going to be an ordinary day. I looked outside and saw the sun was shining. I thought, "Good."

For the first time I *wanted* a game to happen.

I got to breakfast a little early, actually feeling happy.

"Today's the day," Dad announced.

"Right."

"Today you'll really win," chipped in my ma.

"Could be."

My father leaned across the table and gave me a tap. "Winning the last game is what matters. Go out with your head high, Ed."

"And my backside up if I lose?" I wanted to know.

"Ed," said my ma, "don't be so hard on yourself. Your father and I are coming to watch."

"Suit yourselves," I said, and beat it to the bus.

As soon as I got to class Saltz and I collected the T-shirts. "What are you going to do with them?" the others kept asking.

"You picked me as captain, didn't you?"

"Mr. Lester did."

"Well, this time, trust *me*."

When we got all the shirts, Saltz and I sneaked into the home ec room and did what needed to be done. Putting them into a bag so no one would see, we went back to class.

"Just about over," I said.

"I'm almost sorry," confessed Saltz.

"Me too," I said. "And I can't figure out why."

"Maybe it's—the team that loses together, really stays together."

"Right. Not one fathead on the whole team. Do you think we should have gotten a farewell present for Mr. Lester?"

"Like what?"

"A begging cup."

It was hard getting through the day. And it's impossible to know how many people wished me luck. From all I got it was clear they considered me the unluckiest guy in the whole world. I kept wishing I could have banked it for something important.

But the day got done.

It was down in the locker room, when we got ready, that I passed out the T-shirts.

Barish held his up. It was the regular shirt with "S.O.R." on the back. But under it Saltz and I had ironed on press letters. Now they all read:

S.O.R.
LOSERS

Barish's reaction was just to stare. That was my only nervous moment. Then he cracked up, laughing like crazy. And the rest, once they saw, joined in. When Mr. Lester came down he brought Mr. Tillman. We all stood up and turned our backs to them.

"Oh, my goodness," moaned Mr. Lester.

"That's sick," said Mr. Tillman. "Sick!" His happy beads shook furiously.

"It's honest," I said.

"It's defeatest," he yelled.

"Mr. Tillman," I asked, "is that true, about your trying out for pro football?"

He started to say something, then stopped, his mouth open. "Yeah. I tried to make it with the pros, but couldn't."

"So you lost too, right?"

"Yeah," chimed in Radosh, "everyone loses sometime."

"Listen here, you guys," said Mr. Tillman, "it's no fun being rejected."

"Can't it be okay to lose sometimes? You did. Lots do. You're still alive. And we don't dislike you because of that."

"Right. We got other reasons," I heard a voice say. I think it was Saltz.

Mr. Tillman started to say something, but turned and fled.

Mr. Lester tried to give us a few final pointers, like don't touch the ball with our hands, only use feet, things that we didn't always remember to do.

"Well," he said finally, "I enjoyed this."

"You did?" said Porter, surprised.

"Well, not much," he admitted. "I never coached anything before. To tell the truth, I don't know anything about soccer."

"Now you tell us," said Eliscue. But he was kidding. We sort of guessed that before.

Just as we started out onto the field, Saltz whispered to me, "What if we win?"

"With our luck, we will," I said.

And on we went.

19

The Last Game

As we ran onto the field we were met with something like a roar. Maybe the whole school wasn't there. But a lot were. And they were chanting, "Win! Win! Win!"

But when they saw the backs of our shirts, they really went wild. Crazy. And you couldn't tell if they were for us or against us. I mean scary . . .

Oh yes, the game . . .

We had been told that Parkville was a team that hadn't won a game either. They looked it. From the way they kicked the ball around—tried to kick the ball around—it was clear this was going to be a true contest between horribles.

The big difference was their faces. Stiff and tight. You could see, they *wanted* to win. Had to win. We were relaxed and fooling around. Having a grand old time.

Not them.

The ref blew his whistle and called for captains. I went out, shook hands. The Parkville guy was really tense. He kept squeezing his hands, rubbing his face. The whole bit.

The ref said he wanted the usual, a clean, hard game, and he told us which side we should defend. "May the best team win," he said. A believer!

Anyway, we started.

(I know the way this is supposed to work . . . There we are, relaxed, having a good time, not caring really what goes on, maybe by this time, not even sweating the outcome. That should make us, in television land—winners. Especially as it becomes very clear that Parkville is frantic about winning. Like crazy. They have a coach who screams himself red-faced all the time. Who knows. Maybe he's going to lose his job if they lose.)

Well . . .

A lot of things happened that game. There was the moment, just like the first game, when their side, dressed in stunning scarlet, came plunging down our way. Mighty Saltz went out to meet them like a battleship. True to form (red face and wild) he gave a mighty kick, and missed. But he added something new. Leave it to my buddy Saltz. He swung so hard he sat down, sat down on the ball. Like he was hatching an egg.

We broke up at that. So did everyone else. Except the Parkville coach. He was screaming, "Penalty! Penalty!"

So they got the ball. And, it's true, I was laughing so much they scored an easy goal. It was worth it.

"Least you could have done is hatched it," I yelled at Saltz.

"I think they allow only eleven on a team," he yelled back.

Then there was the moment when Porter, Radosh and Dorman got into a really terrific struggle to get the ball—from each other. Only when they looked up did they realize with whom they were struggling. By that time, of course, it was too late. Stolen ball.

There was the moment when Parkville knocked the ball out of bounds. Macht had to throw it in. He snatched up the ball, held it over his head, got ready to heave it, then—dropped it.

It was a close game though. The closest. By the time it was almost over they were leading by only one. We were actually in the game.

And how did the crowd react? They didn't know what to do. Sometimes they laughed. Sometimes they chanted that "Win! Win!" thing. It was like a party for them.

Then it happened . . .

Macht took the ball on a pass from Lifsom. Lifsom dribbled down the right side and flipped it toward the middle. Hays got it fairly well, and, still driving, shot a pass back to Radosh, who somehow managed to snap it easy over to Porter, who was right near the side of the goal.

Porter, not able to shoot, knocked the ball back to Hays, who charged toward the goal—only some Parkville guy managed to get in the way. Hays, screaming, ran right over him, still controlling the ball.

I stood there, astonished. "They've gotten to him," I said to myself. "He's flipped."

I mean, Hays was like a wild man. Not only had he the cleanest shot in the universe, he was desperate.

And so . . . he tripped. Fell flat on his face. Thunk!

Their goalie scooped up the ball, flung it downfield and that was the end of that.

As for Hays, he picked himself up, slowly, too slowly.

The crowd grew still.

You could see it all over Hays. Shame. The crowd waited. They were feeling sorry for him. You could feel it. And standing there in the middle of the field— everything had just stopped—everybody was watching Hays—the poor guy began to cry.

That's all you could hear. His sobs. He had failed.

Then I remembered. "SOR LOSER!" I bellowed.

At my yell, our team snapped up their heads and looked around.

"SOR LOSER!" I bellowed again.

The team picked up the words and began to run

toward Hays, yelling, cheering, screaming, "SOR LOSER! SOR LOSER! SOR LOSER!"

Hays, stunned, began to get his eyes up.

Meanwhile, the whole team, and I'm not kidding, joined hands and began to run in circles around Hays, still giving the chant.

The watching crowd, trying to figure out what was happening, finally began to understand. And they began to cheer!

"SOR LOSER   SOR LOSER   SOR LOSER!"

As for Hays, well, you should have seen his face. It was like a Disney nature-film flower blooming. Slow, but steady. Fantastic! There grew this great grin on his face. Then he lifted his arms in victory and he too began to cheer. He had won—himself.

Right about then the horn blared. The game was over. The season was done. Losers again. Champions of the bloody bottom.

We hugged each other, screamed and hooted like teams do when they win championships. And we were a lot happier than those Parkville guys who had won.

In the locker room we started to take off our uniforms. Mr. Lester broke in.

"Wait a minute," he announced. "Team picture."

We trooped out again, lining up, arm in arm, our *backs* to the camera. We were having fun!

"English test tomorrow," said Saltz as he and I headed for home. "I haven't studied yet. I'll be up half the night."

"Don't worry," I said. "For *that*, I believe in you."

"You know what?" he said. "So do I."

And he did. Aced it. *Our* way.